Lilly
and the
RED SHOES

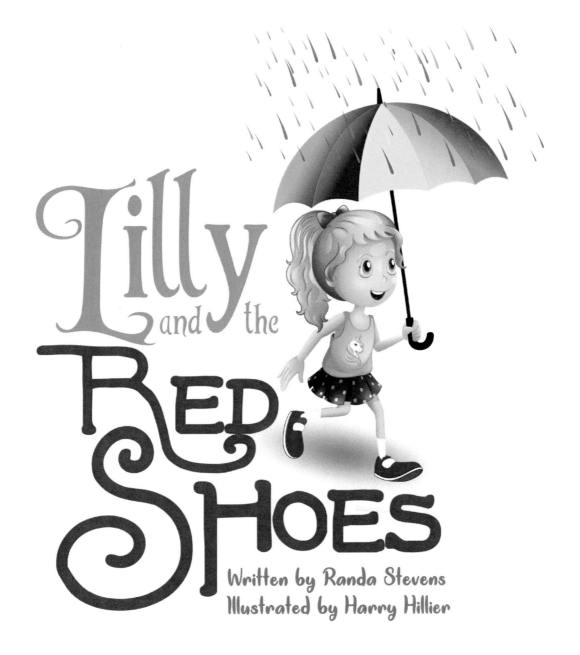

Lilly and the RED SHOES

Written by Randa Stevens

Illustrated by Harry Hillier

Printed in the United States of America.

First Printing, 2020

ISBN: 978-1-951883-33-1

Edited by Madison Lawson
Cover Art, Illustrations, and Layout by Harry Hillier

Butterfly Typeface Publishing
PO Box 56193
Little Rock Arkansas 72215
www.butterflytypeface.com
info@butterflytypeface.com
501-681-0080

Dedication

To my hero Henlea,
    May your tomorrows always be better
                      than your yesterdays.

This is the story
of a beautiful young girl
and her favorite
red shoes...

Lilly was a little girl
the age of five.

She had hair as golden as the sun, and eyes blue like the sky.

Lilly loved to

play,

dance,

and have tea
for two.

And she loved to do it all in
her favorite red shoes.

In her red shoes, Lilly would pick flowers,

skip, hop,

run,

blow bubbles,
and giggle
when they
would POP!

She ate apples and oranges and sometimes sweet treats, but only if she had her red shoes on her feet!

Up with the sun
and off to school she would go

wearing a **red** dress, **red** shoes, and
even a **red** bow.

Lilly went everywhere in her **red shoes**,
except in the rain.

If her shoes got wet,
they would never be the same.

Lilly was getting taller inch by inch. One day, she went to the doctor because she felt a sudden pinch!

The doctor looked in her ears and up her nose. But the problem was Lilly's feet. They were starting to GROW!

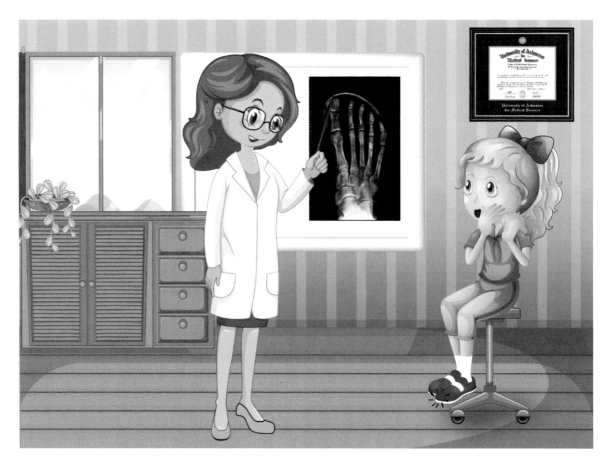

The doctor looked down and noticed Lilly's **red** shoes.
They were scuffed and tattered and very well used.
Shaking her head, she told Lilly the bad news.
"You're a big girl now; you're too big for your shoes."

Lilly pouted and sighed;
her shoulders gave a
small shrug.
She walked out of the
office and wiped her
bare feet on the rug.

The next morning
Lilly's mom gave her a
big, yellow box with a
pretty, pink bow on top.

She opened the box
and what did she
see?

NEW RUBBER BOOTS

PINK POLKA DOT and GREEN!

Lilly liked her new boots, but they
were not quite the same.

Then she laughed,
"Now, I can play in the RAIN.

I can splash in puddles and catch rain in my hand!

I can watch for rainbows, and in the mud, I can stand!"

Lilly loved her red shoes,
and always would
you see,

but now Lilly's favorite shoes were
PINK POLKA DOT
and GREEN!

About the Author

Randa Stevens has a significant place in her heart for special needs children. Her passion is largely in part because of her daughter's incredible and unique journey. The first-time author is also a non-profit volunteer and advocate.

The devoted mother was born and raised in South Arkansas, where she resides with her eleven-year-old daughter.

Made in the USA
Coppell, TX
10 December 2020